# My Little

by

## Adeline Crossland-Rimmington

A little girl learns about
the power of friendship and never gives up
on her quest to find her heart.

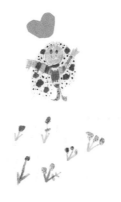

YOUCAXTON
PUBLICATIONS

ISBN 978-1-915972-32-3
Published by YouCaxton Publications 2023

YouCaxton Publications
www.youcaxton.co.uk

For my house bunny.

This book was written when I was five years old. I love to use my imagination to write, draw and tell stories.

*Editor's note:*
When Adeline is not writing or drawing, she enjoys bike riding, climbing, baking, playing with her friends or snuggling with her beloved house bunny.

My little heart, shiny as a star, white and fluffy, shine little heart, shine.

'I want that heart', the girl said. 'I'll get somebody to get it.'

And off she went. Soon she met a man called Joe.

The girl asked Joe to get the heart. They jumped and jumped but they couldn't reach so they went to find somebody else.

They walked and walked until they met a farmer called Max.

Max had a ladder. They hung the ladder on a tree branch. They climbed on the ladder, but they still couldn't reach the heart.

Then they met a fireman called Sam.

Sam had a water-cannon hose. They used it to get the heart, but they still couldn't get the heart.

Then they met a policeman called Sunny. Sunny had a rope.

Sunny threw the rope at the heart, but they still couldn't get the heart.

They walked and walked until they met a fairy called Tinkerbell. Tinkerbell could fly and climb.

She tried and tried but she still couldn't get the heart. She had one last go and....

...she got the heart!

The girl thanked her friends
for all their help.

She gave milk and cookies to everyone, and they all watched TV with the glow of the heart keeping them warm.

## Questions:

Who did the girl ask first to get the heart?

What did the fireman use to get the heart?

Who did Tinkerbell give the heart to - the boy or the girl?

What food did the girl give to her friends?

How special would a heart be to you?

BV - #0061 - 020124 - C28 - 160/133/2 - PB - 9781915972323 - Gloss Lamination